Cannon's Crash Course

Written by Mon Trice

Illustrated by Cbabi Bayoc

Cannon's Crash Course

Published by Red Duck Books,
an imprint of Pageway Publishing

ISBN 978-0-9831631-0-7

Illustrations: Cbabi Bayoc

Book Design: Donna Osborn Clark at Creation By Donna

RED DUCK BOOKS | PAGEWAY PUBLISHING
St. Louis, Missouri 63137

www.montrice.net

Printed in the United States of America

In partnership with

St. Louis
Black Authors
of
Children's Literature

Dedicated to my little brown SONshine.
This book would not exist without you.
Eternal love and gratitude,
Mommy

This book belongs to

_____

St. Louis
Black Authors
of
Children's Literature

Ensuring all children become confident and competent readers by the end of third grade.

When it came to riding his-
he did not have a clue.

He plowed over some daisies
and nearly squashed a pup.

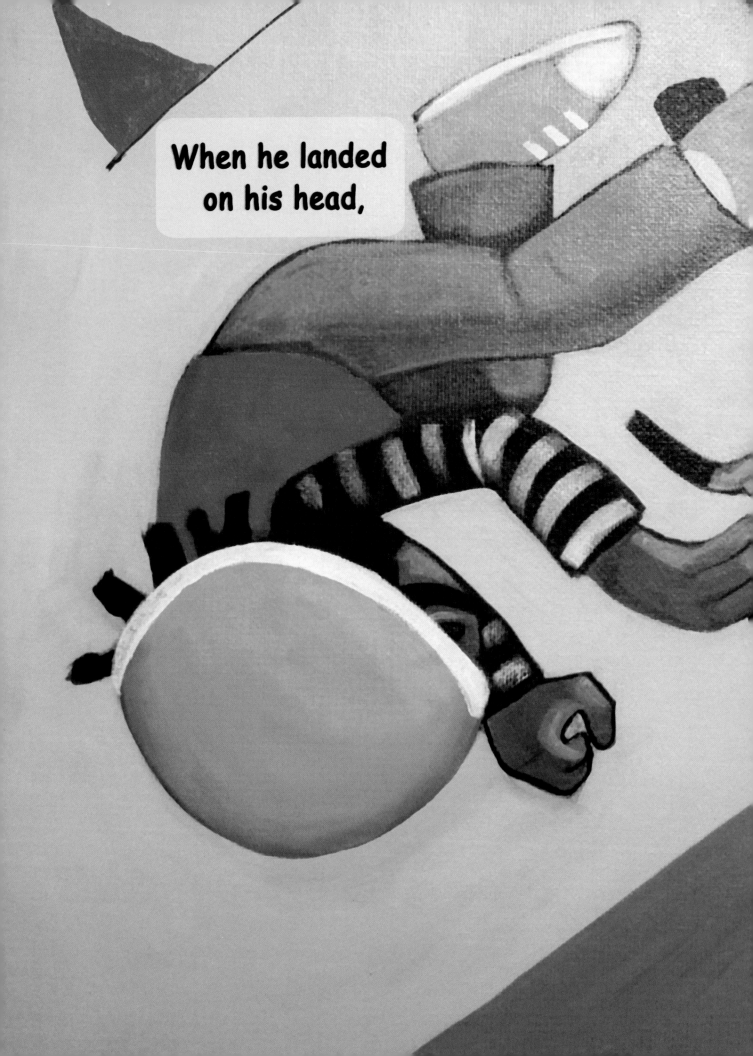

Tee Baker went to help him - pink frosting on his head.

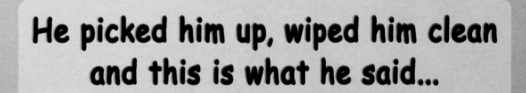

He picked him up, wiped him clean
and this is what he said...

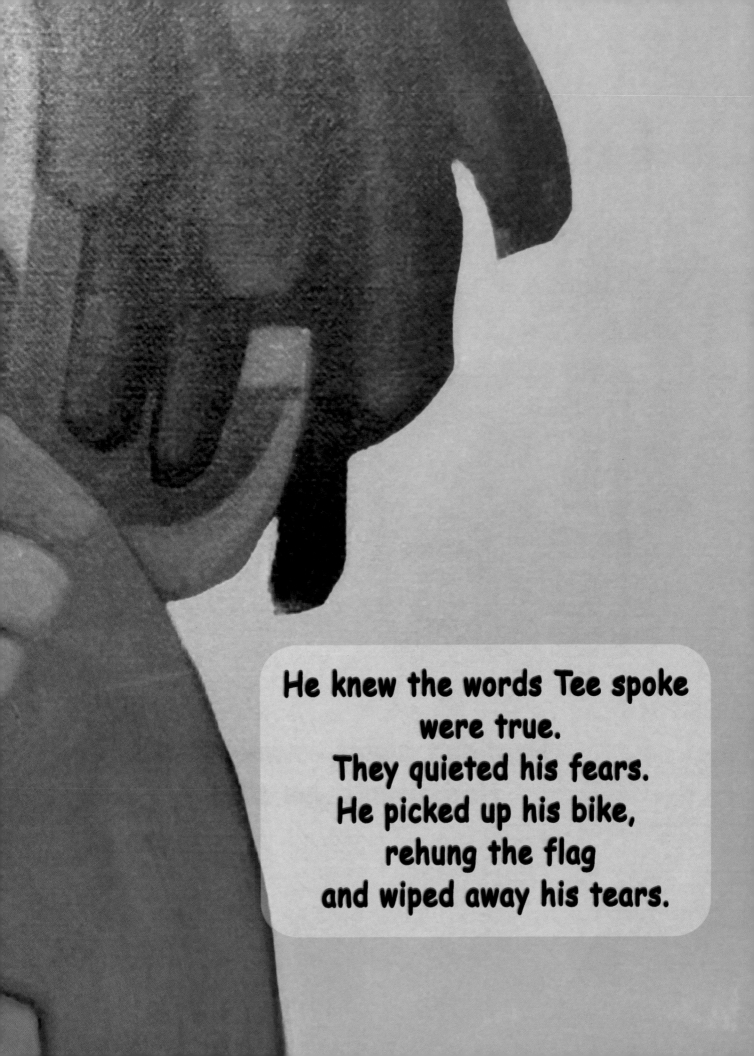

He didn't wiggle or wobble.
He'd given it his all.

In Cannon's heart
he'd not forget
the day he learned
to ride.

The End